Scholastic Canada Ltd.
123 Newkirk Road, Richmond Hill, Ontario, Canada L4C 3G5

Scholastic Inc.
730 Broadway, New York, NY 10003, USA

Ashton Scholastic Pty Limited
PO Box 579, Gosford, NSW 2250, Australia

Ashton Scholastic Limited
Private Bag 1, Penrose, Auckland, New Zealand

Scholastic Publications Ltd.
Villiers House, Clarendon Avenue, Leamington Spa,
Warwickshire CV32 5PR, UK

6 5 4 3   Printed in Hong Kong   3 4 5 6/9

Canadian Cataloguing in Publication Data

Caumartin, François
    [Cachettes et camouflages. English]
    Now you see them, now you don't

Translation of: Cachettes et camouflages.
ISBN 0-590-74035-0

I. Titre. II. Titre: Cachettes et camouflages.
English.

PS8555.A869C3213 1993   jC813'.54   C92-095034-5
PZ7.C386No 1993

NOW YOU SEE THEM, NOW YOU DON'T

François Caumartin

English text by
David Homel

Scholastic Canada Ltd.

Simon was a famous hunter, and he had a collection of trophies from all over the world.

But his collection was not complete.

One day he packed his bags and set off for faraway lands.

From the tropics to the equator, the word went out among the inhabitants. They all wondered what they should do.

The Council of Animals held a meeting and decided to find a way to escape the danger.

"This calls for action," the elephant trumpeted.

"There's strength in numbers," the rhinoceros grunted.

"Let's find a solution!" the lion roared.

No sooner said than done. They took out paint and brushes, and everyone pitched in to find the best hiding places and the cleverest camouflage.

They worked so well that when Simon arrived, he was surprised to find only flowers, rocks and empty fields.

He looked as hard as he could, but there wasn't a wild animal in sight.

He crossed savannas and plains without finding a single wild beast. Not even a rhinoceros. Though he did come across a few cows that glanced at him as he went by . . .

. . . along with some pink flamingos that watched him nervously.

But they were hardly worth the effort for a big-game hunter like Simon!

For days, weeks, months he travelled, through country after country.

He explored a thousand caves, crossed a thousand valleys, beat the bushes along a thousand rivers . . . but it was no use. The land was empty and abandoned.

"Let's look a little deeper in the forest," Simon decided next.

But even in the heart of the jungle Simon found nothing. Discouraged, he leaned against a tree to rest a while.

"I'd better face the facts," he said to himself. "There's no big game to hunt here."

So Simon went home, without having seen a single tiger, elephant, rhinoceros, hippopotamus, crocodile, giraffe or lion.

What a disappointment!

That was a great day for the animals, and they got together for a grand celebration. As a souvenir of Simon's visit, they composed this little refrain:

All you hunters, hear our song,
Don't bother bringing guns along.
Instead of shooting that giraffe,
Why don't you take a photograph?